by David A. Carter

Ready-to-Read

Simon Spotlight
New York   London   Toronto   Sydney   New Delhi

SIMON SPOTLIGHT
An imprint of Simon & Schuster Children's Publishing Division
1230 Avenue of the Americas, New York, New York 10020
This Simon Spotlight edition May 2016
Copyright © 2016 by David A. Carter
All rights reserved, including the right of reproduction in whole or in part in any form.
SIMON SPOTLIGHT, READY-TO-READ, and colophon are registered trademarks of Simon & Schuster, Inc.
For information about special discounts for bulk purchases, please contact
Simon & Schuster Special Sales at 1-866-506-1949 or business@simonandschuster.com.
The Simon & Schuster Speakers Bureau can bring authors to your live event.
For more information or to book an event contact the Simon & Schuster Speakers Bureau at 1-866-248-3049
or visit our website at www.simonspeakers.com.
Manufactured in the United States of America 0416 LAK
10 9 8 7 6 5 4 3 2 1
This book has been cataloged with the Library of Congress.
ISBN 978-1-4814-4050-9 (pbk)
ISBN 978-1-4814-4051-6 (hc)
ISBN 978-1-4814-4052-3 (eBook)

Meet Bitsy Bee
and Busy Bug.
They are best friends.

Today, Bitsy and Busy
are going to a place
they have not been before.

Bitsy packs towels
and toys.
Busy packs buckets, books,
and more!

The Bugs pile into the car.
They go past
the schoolhouse.
They go through town.

They go up a
mountain.
Then they go down.

"Are we there yet?"
asks Bitsy.
"Are we there yet?"
asks Busy.

The car stops.
There is sand.
There are waves.
The Bugs are at the beach.
Yippee!

"Look up," says Bitsy.
Bird Bugs are flying
in the air.

Squawk! Squawk!
Busy smiles.
"Hello up there!"

The friends look
at their beach toys.
What should they make?

"A sand castle!"
cries Busy.
They use shovels, buckets,
and even a little rake.

Bucket after bucket,
it is the biggest
castle in the land!

It has towers,
and a moat, and a
castle wall made of sand!

But then a Bird Bug
swoops down.
It lands on the castle
that is now big and tall.

Uh-oh.
It looks like the castle
is about to fall!

It teeters.
It totters.
It comes down with a crash.

Bitsy and Busy look
at each other.
Then Busy lets
out a laugh.

"We can build
another castle later,"
Busy says.
He points at the sea.

"Let's go down there!"
he tells Bitsy.

The water is
cool and deep and blue.

Surfer Bugs ride the waves.
Swimming Bugs
swim around.
There are Sailing Bugs, too!

Bitsy and Busy
splash about.
"Hooray for the beach!"
they shout.